A MAGIC CIRCLE BOOK

# THE TAIL OF THE MOUSE

retold by **JOAN M. LEXAU**
illustrated by **ROBERTA LANGMAN**

THEODORE CLYMER
SENIOR AUTHOR, READING 360

**XEROX**

GINN AND COMPANY
A XEROX EDUCATION COMPANY

Home Office, Lexington, Massachusetts 02173
Library of Congress Catalog Card Number: 72-97340
0-663-25474-4

# THE TAIL
## OF
## THE MOUSE

The cat bit off the tail of the mouse.

"Give me back my tail," said the mouse.

The cat said, "I'll give you back your tail
if you go to the cow and get me some milk."

Up jumped the mouse and ran.

She ran to the cow and began,

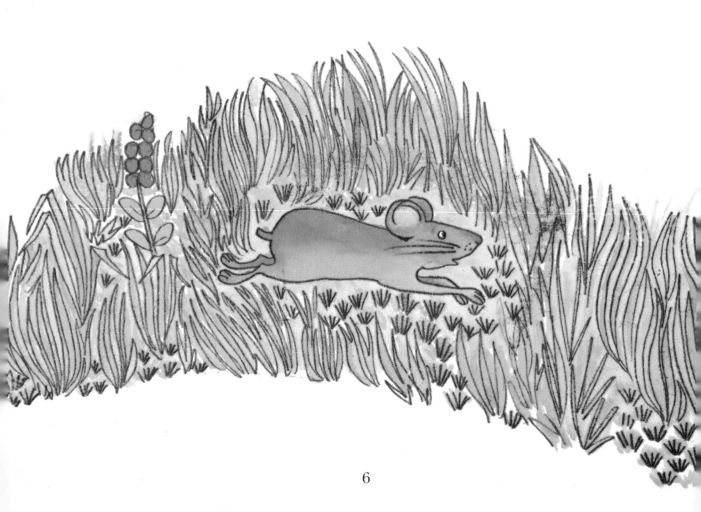

"Please, cow, give me some milk
so I can give milk to the cat
so the cat will give me my tail back."

The cow said, "I'll give you some milk
if you go to the farmer and get me some hay."

Up jumped the mouse and ran.

She ran to the farmer and began,

"Please, farmer, give me some hay

so I can give hay to the cow

so the cow will give me milk

so I can give milk to the cat

so the cat will give me my tail back."


The farmer said, "I'll give you some hay

if you go to the butcher and get me some meat."

Up jumped the mouse and ran.

She ran to the butcher and began,

"Please, butcher, give me some meat

so I can give meat to the farmer

so the farmer will give me hay

so I can give hay to the cow

so the cow will give me milk

so I can give milk to the cat

so the cat will give me my tail back."

The butcher said, "I'll give you some meat
if you go to the baker and get me some bread."

Up jumped the mouse and ran.

She ran to the baker and began,

"Please, baker, give me some bread

so I can give bread to the butcher

so the butcher will give me meat

so I can give meat to the farmer

so the farmer will give me hay

so I can give hay to the cow

so the cow will give me milk

so I can give milk to the cat

so the cat will give me my tail back."


"Yes," said the baker, "I'll give you some bread.
But if you eat my grain, I'll cut off your head."

Then the baker gave the mouse bread

and the mouse gave the bread to the butcher

and the butcher gave the mouse meat

and the mouse gave the meat to the farmer

and the farmer gave the mouse hay

and the mouse gave the hay to the cow

and the cow gave the mouse milk

and the mouse gave the milk to the cat.

And the cat gave the mouse her tail back.

BCDEFGHIJK  7654
PRINTED IN THE UNITED STATES OF AMERICA